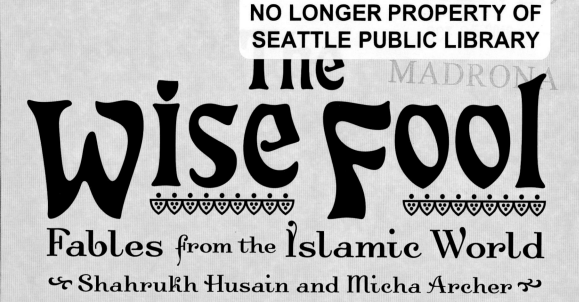

The Wise Fool

Fables from the Islamic World

∾ Shahrukh Husain and Micha Archer ❧

Barefoot Books
step inside a story

❧ Contents ❧

Introduction

I can't recall when I heard my first Mulla Nasruddin tale, or who told it to me. All I remember is that wherever I went as a child in India or Pakistan, everyone knew him. As I grew up, he remained a central character in my world of stories, a merry little figure with a turban and short jacket and a much-loved donkey.

Then I realised that the people of many countries shared the Mulla's stories. His tales were told right across the Islamic world and surrounding areas – from the Arab Middle East to Turkey, Afghanistan, Iran, Greece, Bulgaria, Macedonia, Albania, parts of Russia and even China. More recently, through the revival of storytelling, the Mulla has travelled to the western world and is now known and loved in Canada, Australia, England and America.

Mulla Nasruddin is sometimes called Khoja (or one of its variations, Hodja, Hoja, Khwaja), which is a term of respect, roughly translated as 'sir' or 'master'. His stories tell of his funny antics and his amusing ways but at the same time, we learn that he is unusually wise. From peasant to emperor, all turn to him for advice. But Nasruddin doesn't have much time for flattery or fakery and often makes a joke of his fame. He also excels at puncturing the vanity of others. Even as a judge, he does not take life or himself seriously. We see him at his most comfortable labouring – or relaxing – in the fields, talking to his donkey, or having cups of coffee with his friends in the market.

Nasruddin has a grumpy side, too. He dislikes boastfulness, laziness, cruelty and arrogance and is often impertinent, even to the emperor, in a way that no one else dares. Rather like a jester, he acts as the social and spiritual conscience of his community and pays little attention to status. In fact, by turning himself into a figure of fun, Mulla Nasruddin brings attention to the problems of a society where open criticism can result in cruel executions. When the Mulla is outspoken or rebellious, he makes his point without getting into trouble.

Over the years, people have added to the Mulla's stories. Similar tales turn up in the folklore of Spain, Ireland and even the Appalachians. Mulla Nasruddin is the familiar folktale character known as a 'wise fool' – someone whose words and actions may appear silly at first but if examined carefully will definitely reveal some wisdom tucked away inside. All of these factors combine to make his stories interesting and thought-provoking both to adults and children.

So who is Mulla Nasruddin? Was he a real person or is he entirely fictional? His origins are uncertain but he is generally thought to have been a travelling Sufi (spiritual seeker), born in a Turkish village called Sivrihisar in Eskisheher in the thirteenth century. It is believed that he wrote at least one book, which was discovered in 1571. Between travels, he lived in Akshehir first and later in Konya. His stories tell us he often stopped in the town of Bursa. The International Festival of Nasruddin Hodja is still held every summer in Akshehir.

Unlike other wise fools, Mulla Nasruddin is a character who develops and changes. In some stories, he is well off; in others, he is out of work and poor. We see him in good moods and bad moods, working and at leisure. But we know him essentially as a loveable, shrewd and jovial character.

Nasruddin can teach us if we wish to learn, and he can always make us laugh.

May he always have the answers to our questions.

Shahrukh Husain

The Price of Steam

Once, when Mulla Nasruddin was a judge, two men came to his court. One was a shopkeeper, large, sturdy and very angry. The other was an old pauper. He was very frail and he was very frightened.

'This man owes me money!' said the shopkeeper. 'Your Honour, you must order him to pay me.'

'But how can I owe you money?' asked the old man. 'I didn't buy anything from you.'

'Tell me your story,' the Mulla said, 'and I will decide what this shopkeeper is owed.'

'Well,' began the old man, 'I was looking for something to eat . . .'

'. . . which does not mean you have the right to steal from me!' shouted the shopkeeper. 'After all, I live by cooking and selling food. I can't let every beggar come and pilfer from my cooking pots, or I'd be joining you in the street.'

'You will have your turn!' said Mulla Nasruddin, looking stern. 'This is a court of law. Kindly do not interrupt again.'

'There is a difference,' said the old man, 'between a beggar and a pauper. I have never begged.' He turned to Mulla Nasruddin. 'I found a piece of bread on the street. I picked it up, but it was too hard to eat. So I walked

to the market to see if I could find something to soften it with. By the side of
the road, outside this gentleman's shop, I saw several cooking pots. They were
bubbling and steaming and a wonderful aroma came wafting out of them. So I
held small pieces of my bread in the steam to make them softer, and the smell
of the meat and herbs allowed me to imagine I was eating something delicious.
When I had finished eating, I thanked this gentleman, and I was about to leave
when he grabbed me by the arm and asked me for money.'

The shopkeeper pounced on the old man's words. 'You admit you enjoyed the delicious
flavours of my food, and yet you refuse to pay me.'

'What would you consider a fair price?' asked the Mulla.

'I'm not a greedy man,' the shopkeeper said. 'Two piastres would be enough.'

Mulla Nasruddin reached into his pocket and took out two coins. He held them up and
jangled them loudly. The shopkeeper's eyes lit up. He stretched out his hand. 'Khoja, you are
a just man.'

'I hope I am, I hope I am,' said Nasruddin, jangling the coins again. 'Now, listen very
carefully, because the sound of these coins is payment for the steam from your food. That's a
fair exchange, I believe, for a miser like you!'

Star Talk

One summer's evening, when the air was balmy and the stars hung bright in the skies, the men of Akshehir sat outside, sipping delicious coffee from tiny glass cups. They were relaxing after a hard day's work, speaking of this and that, and the conversation eventually drifted to the stars above. Some of the men believed that the stars showed what kind of person you were, or could even tell humankind what lay in the future.

'So, Khoja,' asked Yunus, 'which star were you born under?'

Mulla Nasruddin took another sip of his coffee, enjoying the fragrance of the crushed cardamom seeds that flavoured it. 'It was a long time ago,' he replied after a few moments, 'but I'm sure it was the Lamb. Yes, that's right. I clearly remember my mother telling me it was the sign of the Lamb.'

The men began to laugh.

'There's no such sign,' said Yunus. 'Don't you mean the Ram?'

Nasruddin put down his cup and gazed at the starry sky. 'It's forty years since my horoscope was cast,' he replied. 'That lamb must surely have grown into a ram by now.'

9

Boys' Games

Mulla Nasruddin walked along the fields on his way home from the mosque. It was Eid-ul-Adha, the Festival of Sacrifice. He thought about a time long ago, when history had not been invented and people remembered everything through stories. The Mulla loved stories. He loved the way they brought events to life.

As he walked, he saw a group of boys playing ball and stopped to watch them.

'Salaam, Khoja,' they shouted, pausing their game. 'Will you play too?'

The Mulla laughed. 'Thank you,' he replied, 'but I'm too old to run about like you youngsters. Though I swear, if my old body could keep up, I would join in.'

The boys gathered round the Mulla. 'It is the festival tomorrow,' they said. 'Tell us the story of Ibrahim and Ismail.'

The Mulla was pleased to be asked. He straightened his turban and began to tell them the story of how God commanded the prophet Ibrahim to sacrifice the life of his only son, Ismail. With a heavy heart, Ibrahim closed his eyes and did as he was told – but when he opened his eyes again, he saw that it was a goat he had sacrificed and not his son. So he passed God's test with flying colours.

'Such is the Grace of God!' said Mulla Nasruddin. 'And do you know, that story is told by people all over the world?'

The boys clustered closer around the Mulla. 'So it was a goat's head and not his son's head that Ibrahim cut off?'

'That's right,' the Mulla replied.

'Aren't heads and turbans more or less the same thing?' said another boy.

The Mulla looked at the cheeky faces around him, and decided it was time to walk on. As he turned to go on his way, he felt a sudden rush of air as his turban was snatched from his head. The next moment, the boys were running about the field, tossing it from one to another. Mulla Nasruddin ran after them, shouting angrily, chasing them up and down as fast as his old legs would go.

'Lost your head, have you, Mulla?' the boys teased as his turban whirled past him, again and again and again. 'Is this your sacrifice for the festival?'

At last Mulla Nasruddin saw the funny side. He wasn't sure he wanted his turban back now. After the way it had been treated, it was grimy and dirty and not fit to be worn. He tidied himself up and began his trek back home.

As he entered the square where he lived, people noticed his turban was missing.

'What happened, Khoja?' asked his nosy neighbour, Enver.

The Mulla replied, 'Oh, I passed some boys playing in the field – and guess what? My turban remembered what it is like to be young and decided to stay and join in.'

Nasruddin's Haircut

Mulla Nasruddin walked through the door of a barber's shop and asked for his head to be shaved.

'Please sit down, Khoja,' the barber said, sharpening his razors and getting down to the task.

'Ouch!' yelped Mulla Nasruddin, soon after the barber began. The barber had nicked his skin.

'Sorry, Khoja,' said the barber, pinching off a piece of cotton wool and sticking it to the cut.

A while later, Nasruddin felt another sharp pain on his scalp. The barber had nicked him a second time.

'What have I got myself into?' thought the Mulla with a wince. 'This man's going to skin me alive!'

The barber pinched off another bit of cotton wool, pasted it to the cut and continued shaving.

'Perhaps he's settling down now,' the Mulla thought. 'He just needed to get going. . .*aaaooo!*'

'So very sorry, Khoja,' the barber stuttered. 'Just wait a moment, and I will put a piece of cotton wool over this cut too.'

'Is there a problem with my head, my man?' asked the Mulla. 'I mean, is it especially bumpy?'

'Of course not, Khoja,' the man muttered, apologising again and again as he began to shave the Mulla's head once more.

But the barber's hand simply didn't settle down. When Mulla Nasruddin felt the razor nick his scalp for a fourth time, he leapt out of his chair and rushed to the door.

'Khoja, wait!' called the barber. 'I haven't finished the job!'

'You've sowed half my head with cotton wool,' the Mulla yelled back. 'I'll sow the rest with a crop of my choice!'

Lying Donkey

'Salaam, Mulla Nasruddin. May God bring down his blessings on you!' called Hamid loudly.

Mulla Nasruddin had dozed off in the winter sun after a hard morning's work. He had been digging and planting, fixing and mending, all according to his wife Fatime's instructions. He felt grumpy about being woken up from such a delicious sleep – and also a little embarrassed to be caught napping by his neighbour.

'And salaam to you,' he said, rising to his feet and hurrying back to his chores.

'You've certainly done lots of hard work this morning, Khoja,' Hamid said, strolling over to stand beside him.

'I certainly have,' replied the Mulla, making a big show of being busy. Hamid was not good news. He was always after a favour, and all his greetings and blessings and compliments worried the Mulla, because they surely meant that he had come to ask for a *big* favour today. Once, he had borrowed a cart from the Mulla and returned it months later with a broken wheel. Another time, he'd asked the schoolteacher for a book, and then followed the poor man about like a shadow, bursting into his classroom and even waking him up at night to make the teacher explain the bits he didn't understand.

'Oh no!' the Mulla thought to himself. 'I'm giving you nothing, my man, because you don't know the meaning of respect.'

'I would love to help you out with this work,' Hamid said, 'but I can hardly get through my own.'

'Here it comes,' thought the Mulla, picking up an axe to hack at a log. The racket of it would block out Hamid's voice and he could pretend not to hear his request.

Hamid took a step closer and yelled over the noise of the chopping axe, 'That's why I've come to you, Khoja. I wanted to borrow your donkey.'

The Mulla was so shocked by this boldness that he forgot to pretend he couldn't hear. 'My donkey? You want to borrow my donkey?'

Everyone knew that the Mulla used his donkey every single day, and that it was more like a friend or a child to him than an animal.

'Yes, Khoja. I'd be very grateful.'

'Well, I. . .' replied the Mulla, trying desperately to think of a way to refuse. What if Hamid broke the donkey's leg, just as he'd broken the wheel of the cart? Or what if Hamid haunted him all day long, asking how he could make the donkey do this, that or the other? Oh no, he wouldn't put himself or the donkey through any of that! Hamid could complain about his meanness, but if it was one fault to refuse the favour, it would be a hundred faults to agree to it.

'So, Khoja,' said Hamid eagerly. 'What do you say?'

Mulla Nasruddin decided that a white lie was in order.

'I'm sorry, my man,' the Mulla said. 'I have already lent the donkey to someone else.'

'Well, perhaps I can borrow it when it comes back?' the man insisted. 'Will it be back today, or maybe tomorrow?'

'Well,' said the Mulla, trying to be polite and wishing he hadn't started this lie. 'I'm not sure when it will be back. You see. . .'

Heeee-haw. Heeee-haw. The loud braying of the donkey interrupted the Mulla.

'Khoja!' Hamid said, looking offended. 'You haven't lent the animal out at all! The donkey's braying tells me that you've been lying to me.'

The Mulla was furious now. He straightened his back and stared the man in the face.

'You believe the braying of a donkey above my word?' he demanded angrily. 'Go away! I'm not going to lend you anything.'

Across the River

Mulla Nasruddin was fishing. It was peaceful by the river and he was looking forward to taking home a couple of plump fish to cook for dinner. Of course, if he caught a few more, he could invite the neighbours round to eat. And if he caught a big basketful, he could ask the whole neighbourhood.

'Oi!' A shout disturbed his peaceful daydreaming. 'Can you hear me?'

A man was waving from the opposite riverbank. 'How can I get to the other side of the river?' he called. 'There are no ferry boats here.'

Mulla Nasruddin looked up without moving his rod. 'I don't know why you need a ferry boat,' the Mulla replied. 'You're already on the other side of the river.'

The Sweetest Poison

Mulla Nasruddin had just finished teaching his class at his religious school, the Madrasah, and was about to leave to deal with some other business.

'Excuse me, Mulla Nasruddin,' said a man, running up to him as he stepped out of the school office. 'My master has sent you these sweets and told me to give them to you personally with a message.'

The Mulla accepted the tray, which was heavy with crispy baklawa. The sweet, tasty pastry was studded with nuts, soaked in honey and fragrant with rosewater. It was the finest, freshest, lightest baklawa he had ever seen. And here he was, about to go out, with no time to eat it!

'What is your master's message, my man?' asked the Mulla, licking his lips.

'My master sends you his deepest praise and gratitude. He has been testing his son, Master Hasan, on your lessons, and he is highly impressed with what you've taught the boy. These sweets are a small way of thanking you.' The man bowed low and hurried off again.

By now, a number of Mulla Nasruddin's pupils had gathered round to see what was going on, and the Mulla knew that the moment he left, they would sneak into his office and steal his baklawa. He couldn't let that happen! He quickly thought up a plan.

'I'm leaving these baklawa in my office,' said the Mulla loudly. 'I'm not going to taste them, even though they're the freshest, most delicious-looking pastries I've ever seen.'

'Why not, Mulla?' asked Ejaz, a bold boy and the Mulla's nephew. 'My mother says you will go anywhere for a good piece of baklawa!'

'Your mother is right,' replied the Mulla. 'I have been known to go to great lengths to get my hands on it. But the thing is. . .' He lowered his head and beckoned to them. The boys clustered round him. 'Now, don't breathe a word to anyone about this, but I happen to know that the man who sent these is a bad man. He has wanted to kill me ever since the day I ruled against him in a court of law. I'm certain that these sweets are poisoned.'

'Throw them away, Mulla!' the boys chorused.

The Mulla looked shocked. 'Have I taught you no sense?' he asked. 'If I throw them away, some starving beggar might eat them.'

'Bury them in the rubbish heap, Uncle!' said Ejaz.

'What? And let them poison some innocent animal foraging for a meal? No, it's safest to leave them in my office until I work out how to get rid of them safely.' He looked at Ejaz. 'You are responsible for making sure no one poisons himself.'

'That clever little trick has sharpened my wits,' the Mulla chuckled to himself as he left the school and went about his business. 'I will negotiate well today.'

The Mulla was right. His mind was alert and he made good, quick deals. He was soon hurrying back to his office at the Madrasah to gorge on the wonderful treat waiting for him. Instead, he found his nephew writhing in agony on the floor of the office, with the other boys crowding around him.

'You greedy rascal!' said the Mulla, looking at the empty tray where the honeyed baklawa had been. 'You just wouldn't listen, would you?'

He went to his desk and slumped into his chair. And then he noticed that his inkpot had been smashed.

'What exactly has been going on?' he demanded.

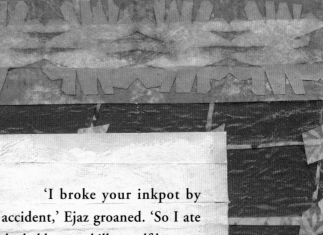

'I broke your inkpot by accident,' Ejaz groaned. 'So I ate the baklawa to kill myself because I was so ashamed and afraid.'

Mulla Nasruddin stood up, shaking his head. 'Try that story again,' he said, 'but in the right order this time.'

'I don't know what you mean, Uncle,' Ejaz stammered.

'Well, how about this version?' said the Mulla. 'The moment I walked out of the Madrasah, leaving you to guard the sweets, you told your friends that I had invented a little story to save the baklawa for myself. You all went in and guzzled my present. Then you started to worry that you'd be punished. So you, Ejaz, smashed my pot and made up your own story to escape punishment. Am I right?'

'Yes, Uncle,' said Ejaz, slowly getting up from the floor. The boys hung their heads, waiting to hear how they would be punished.

'This time,' said the Mulla, 'there will be no punishment. Ejaz was so desperate for the sweets that he concocted a tale to have them – just as I did. And besides, I'm delighted that he has inherited my talent for telling stories.'

Is It Possible?

The Emperor Taimur summoned Mulla Nasruddin to the royal court.

'Ah, Mulla,' he said. 'I want you to meet these three wise scholars. They have travelled the world, and they claim that no man knows what they do not. I've told them you can tell them something they don't know. I hope you can, Mulla, because you have seen what happens to those who let me down.'

The Mulla gulped.

'Well, Mulla?' Taimur asked. 'What do you say?'

'Your Majesty,' said Mulla Nasruddin, 'must I enter this competition? I have not travelled the world, nor do I claim to know a lot about it.'

Taimur laughed. 'I know you will produce something from that head of yours to save it from being chopped off.'

He signalled to the three wise scholars and they stepped forward.

'How many stars are there in the sky?' asked the first scholar.

'As many as the hairs on my donkey,' replied the Mulla.

'How can you be so sure?' asked the first scholar.

'Count them and you'll see,' the Mulla snapped.

The first scholar stepped back.

'How many hairs are there in my beard?' asked the second scholar.

'Exactly the same number as there are in my donkey's tail,' replied the Mulla.

'How can you prove that?' challenged the second scholar.

'Personally, I need no proof,' said Mulla Nasruddin. 'But if you do, you are very welcome to fetch my donkey and count them yourself.'

Scholar number three pursed his lips and furrowed his brow. He stroked his beard, then folded his hands and spoke with a high and mighty air.

'But is it possible, my friend, to count the hairs in a donkey's tail?'

And the Mulla replied, 'Is it possible, my friend, to count the stars in the sky?'

Predicting the Future

'If you don't trim the branches of that tree outside,' said Mulla Nasruddin's wife, Fatime, one morning, 'I will pay someone to come and do it.'

The Mulla hated wasting money.

'Why complain?' he demanded. 'It's a tree. It's a tree's job to grow and put out branches.'

'Yes, but I don't want it blocking the windows of my house and turning day into night!'

Mulla Nasruddin wrinkled up his eyes and peered through the window. He had to admit, he could not have guessed from inside that the sun was shining so gloriously outside. So he hoisted his saw onto his back and climbed the tree.

'Nag, nag, nag,' he muttered, crawling along a sturdy branch to its outer edge.

He sawed its end off and sat back to survey the effect. Better, but not nearly enough. His wife was right. The thick leaves of the tree hung directly over the windows. He manoeuvred his saw this way and that way, but his position was awkward and the leafier branches were just out of reach.

The Mulla looked again. 'If I were to sit over there, I could reach the thickest leaves; and once I have trimmed them off, my body would mark exactly where I need to saw through the main branch.'

He braced himself and edged forwards a few inches at a time until he had shuffled to where he wanted to be. The main branch was steady, so he crouched flat, clinging to it with both arms, and turned himself round to face the tree trunk. When he was safely astride, he sat up, grasped his saw and began cutting through the leafy branches.

'Salaam, Mulla Nasruddin!' a neighbour yelled up. 'Good morning! You're working very early.'

'As the day demands,' replied the Mulla. 'You know the morning call to prayer tells us "Prayer is better than sleep". And work is a kind of prayer, so here I am.'

He turned back to his sawing.

'Oh, Mulla!' the man called again.

'I don't wish to be rude, my friend,' snapped the Mulla, 'but this is not the time for chit-chat. I must concentrate on my task or I could hurt myself.'

'That's just what I'm worried about,' said the man. 'Do you know you're sitting on the wrong side of that big branch? When you saw through it, you'll fall.'

And the Mulla replied, 'Well, thank you for your warning, my dear man. But I know exactly what I'm doing.'

Mulla Nasruddin continued to saw. Finally, he looked down at the ground and saw a fine mound of leafy branches. He got to work on the main branch now, thinking of a nice cool wash before he sat down to an enjoyable breakfast – because, surely, Fatime would have a hearty meal waiting to reward him for his hard early-morning labours.

SNAP! CRASH! Suddenly the Mulla was tumbling through the air, landing with a thump on the pile of leafy branches. He looked again and saw his legs still astride the biggest branch. Forgetting his bruises and scratches, he leapt up and ran straight into his neighbour's house.

'My friend!' he yelled excitedly. 'I've lived next door to you all this time, and you've never told me you can predict the future!'

Bread and Salt

The Mulla was on business in Bursa and, after a long day, he was ready for a fine meal before going to bed.

'Can one of you gentlemen point me to a respectable rest house?' he asked a small crowd of people who were gathered in the street.

A man stepped forward. 'Allow me to offer you some hospitality, Mulla,' he said. The Mulla was embarrassed. 'I can't intrude on you,' he said. 'I am a travelling man. I'm used to eating and sleeping at inns.'

'No trouble at all,' the man insisted. 'You have made a good impression on me, and I would appreciate the chance to speak to you some more.'

The Mulla hesitated. To refuse again would be rude. 'Well then,' he said, 'thank you. I will accompany you for some bread and salt. I don't want to put you to any trouble.'

His host seated him at the dining table and disappeared into the kitchen. A few moments later, he reappeared with a small loaf of bread and a large bowl.

'Broth!' thought Nasruddin. He could almost taste the warm liquid slipping down his throat.

But the bowl was filled with rough grains of salt. Disappointed, the Mulla contented himself with sprinkling the salt onto the loaf of bread, washing it down with plenty of water so that he would not be thirsty all night.

'Well,' he thought, 'we all know that asking for bread and salt is just a polite way of accepting an invitation – but even so, I brought this on myself.'

Just then a beggar called in at the window, 'Please sir, spare some food and drink for a starving man.'

The Mulla's host ignored the cries of the beggar.

'Spare some bread and salt for a poor man,' wailed the beggar again.

Excusing himself, the Mulla leapt from the table and ran to the window.

'I advise you to move on to the next house, my friend,' he whispered, 'My host is a man of his word. If you ask him for bread and salt, that's exactly what you'll get.'

Where It Belongs

Mulla Nasruddin was very thirsty. He squinted into the night, trying to see if he could spot the lights of a town in the distance, but all was dark and quiet.

'I hope,' he thought, 'that I can find some water soon.'

A gust of wind blew in his direction, so he pulled his cloak tightly around him and looked up at the sky. Heavy clouds kept hiding the moon and stars, telling him that the rain was sure to start soon.

'Merciful Lord,' he cried, 'I know I prayed for water – I don't want to be ungrateful, but that's not what I meant!'

He had hardly finished speaking when he bumped hard into what felt like a low stone wall. He fumbled at it, trying to work out what he had found.

'A well!' he gasped, catching hold of a rope that hung down into the water. The Mulla glanced over the wall and into the depths of the well. There, glimmering up at him, was the moon, round and fat and shiny.

'So there you are!' the Mulla yelled down. 'How is a traveller meant to continue his journey if you don't stay in the sky?'

The Mulla tied a large hook to the end of the rope and cast it into the water, swinging it this way and that to try and capture the moon. At last, the hook snagged on a rock sticking out from the side of the well.

'Now I've caught you!' sang the Mulla in delight. He pulled at the rope, trying his hardest to draw up the moon. At last he gave a mighty tug, and the hook slipped off the stone and flew upwards out of the well. The Mulla staggered backwards and fell onto the ground, his eyes closed, gasping for breath. When he opened his eyes, he saw the moon shining down on him from the great, star-filled sky – just as round and fat and shiny as it had looked in the well.

'Ah! Thank goodness!' he exclaimed. 'I may have had a bad fall, but at least I've got the moon back in the sky where it belongs.'

33

A Fair Reward

Mulla Nasruddin had travelled for days. He was tired and dusty and his bones felt sore. He distracted himself by imagining wonderful places and hospitable people who gave him delicious food, steaming hot and fragrant. Thinking of the things he loved made the road seem shorter. As he trudged along, his mind lingering on his favourite things, he arrived at the gates of a large town.

'That worked well,' he thought. 'My thoughts gave me wings.'

The Mulla walked on, his eyes scanning all the buildings, until finally he arrived at the doors of a smart-looking bath house. As he pushed them open, two attendants came forward to meet him.

'I'm a stranger in town,' the Mulla said to them. 'I've been travelling for days and I'm desperate for a bath.'

'We can see that,' the attendants muttered.

They looked him up and down, nudging each other at the sight of his shabby clothes and his torn shoes. When the Mulla took off his turban, they raised their eyebrows at his matted hair. When he removed his shoes, they held their noses as if to say his feet were smelly. The Mulla ignored them, as he always ignored bad behaviour, and stood waiting until finally they handed him a bit of dried-up soap and a worn, tattered towel. Then he plunged himself into the bath.

The water was warm and, as he bathed, he could feel his weariness wash away. The water carried his weight and lapped around him, his muscles began to relax, and the aching in his tired bones eased.

When at last he was done, Mulla Nasruddin got out of the water, and returned the towel and what was left of the soap. Then he dropped a shining gold coin into the hand of each attendant. The men stared, rubbing the coins to see if they were imagining things.

'Only a fool would reward someone for such poor service,' said one. 'What would he give us if we paid him more attention?'

'Let's just hope we get that chance,' said the other.

'Oh you will, you will,' the Mulla resolved as he stepped into the fresh air outside.

A week later, Mulla Nasruddin returned to the bath house. The two attendants recognised him immediately, and this time they behaved very differently. They smiled and bowed. They gave him thick, soft towels decorated with dainty stitches, and a loincloth of the softest satin. They fetched the finest loofahs, kept especially for the town's nobles, and they scrubbed and rubbed his body before massaging him with exquisite, healing oils.

When the Mulla had been cleaned and pampered to his satisfaction, he dressed himself and turned to reward them. He pressed a coin into each of their hands and stood back. The men opened their hands with excitement – but then their faces fell. On each palm lay the tiniest copper coin you could find.

'What's this?' stammered the two men in shock.

And the Mulla replied, 'This is for last week. The gold coins were for today.'

Magic Money

A crowd of people clustered around a stall in the market place. Mulla Nasruddin edged his way to the front to see what was attracting the crowd.

'This is a very special sword,' the salesman yelled, 'and it only costs three thousand piastres.'

'You could buy fifteen donkeys for that amount. And you can buy a sword like that for a hundredth of the price,' said a man from the crowd. 'What's so special about this one?'

'You've misunderstood, my friend,' the Mulla joked. 'It is the price that makes this sword special, not the other way round.'

'Everything is a joke to you, Mulla,' the salesman said. 'But let me tell you, my friends, this sword may not look like anything special here, in a market place, in times of peace. But take it to war and you will see its magic.'

The crowd clamoured to find out more.

'In battle,' the salesman said, drawing the sword from its scabbard, 'the user pulls it out to attack his enemy – like so. And this sword, no more than three feet long as you look at it now, will stretch instantly to five feet.' He raised his arm so that the sword swayed and glinted high above his head. 'That, my friends, is the miracle of this sword. It is a magic sword.'

The crowd cheered and clapped, and the Mulla was impressed at the man's selling skills, especially when one of the crowd stepped forward and bought the sword.

'He certainly knows the magic of creating money,' thought the Mulla as he walked home. The following week, he went along to the market and found the same salesman.

'I have something for you to sell,' he said, handing over a metal object. 'I want three thousand piastres for it.'

The salesman unwrapped the Mulla's parcel.

'Excuse me, Mulla, but why are you asking so much for a pair of kitchen tongs?'

The Mulla looked surprised. 'Last week you sold a sword for the same price – and it wasn't even new.'

'But Mulla, much as I respect you, I have to say that this is a very ordinary pair of tongs – I sell them myself for less than three piastres.'

'Last week, you managed to sell a very ordinary sword for a vast price. Most people would say you created money from nothing.'

'You forget, Mulla, that was a magic sword. In battle it extended. . .'

'. . .from three feet to five. Yes, I remember. And when my wife hurls these tongs in domestic battle, my friend, they fly through the air to a distance of ten feet – that means that in action, they go twice the length of the sword.'

Food for Growing

Mulla Nasruddin slipped quietly into the courtroom and took a seat at the side. Emperor Taimur had made him a judge, and he felt there was a lot to be learnt from watching others at work.

The judge arrived and took his seat.

'I've seen this man before,' the Mulla thought. 'But where?'

Before he could remember, the case began.

'My Lord Judge,' began a well-dressed merchant, 'I often pass Akshehir on business, and when I travel to and fro, I spend the night at the rest house belonging to this man.' He pointed to an innkeeper, a hunched, angry-looking man who was standing not far from the Mulla.

'The last time I was on my way to Istanbul, I had a meal at his rest house. Before I went to my room, I told him I would be leaving early in the morning, and I promised to pay the bill on my way back home. He agreed. When I had finished my business in Istanbul, I returned to the rest house and asked for my account. And to my surprise, he presented me with a bill for two hundred piastres! That's enough to feed my donkey for a year.'

'Were you satisfied with the food and the room?' the judge asked.

'I was indeed, Your Honour.'

'Then what is your complaint?'

'Your Honour, two hundred piastres is not a fair price for only two visits! Surely anyone can see that.'

The judge turned to the innkeeper. 'What have you to say, my man?'

'Each time he visited, Your Honour, I gave him a hearty meal of a chicken, two eggs and half a loaf of bread.'

'Generous, I'll agree,' the judge said, 'but the price still seems high.'

'Well you see, Your Honour,' said the innkeeper, 'this gentleman did not pay me immediately and he returned three whole months later. During that time, the chicken he ate could have laid ninety eggs. And those ninety eggs would have hatched into chickens and been ready to lay eggs themselves by now. In fact, I would have had a whole coop full of chickens, each one laying dozens of eggs. . .you must appreciate that I could have made much more than two hundred piastres from the chicken this customer ate.'

The judge nodded. His face was serious.

Mulla Nasruddin pushed back his turban a tiny fraction and looked at him from beneath furrowed brows. And then he remembered where he had seen the judge before – leaving the house of the innkeeper, thanking him for his excellent meal, while a little boy followed him carrying a very fat, freshly roasted goose. The Mulla frowned more deeply and concentrated hard.

The judge cleared his throat. 'After reflecting carefully on the accounts from both sides,' he said, 'I have decided that the innkeeper has the better case. The merchant is to pay the full two hundred piastres here and now.'

'But Your Honour. . .' the merchant protested.

'But me no buts,' the judge snapped. 'It is decided.'

'Then we will appeal the case,' a voice called from the side of the room.

'Who said that?' the judge demanded.

Mulla Nasruddin rose slowly to his feet and ambled over to the centre of the courtroom. 'If this worthy gentleman will accept my help, that is.'

The merchant accepted, and a few weeks later the case came to court again. But there was no sign of Mulla Nasruddin. The innkeeper fidgeted with his accounts, the merchant stood waiting, the judge grew impatient, the officers of the court looked anxious, and the spectators whispered and shuffled. But still the Mulla didn't come.

The judge had had enough. 'Bring Mulla Nasruddin here!' he commanded. 'How dare he keep us waiting?'

Just at that moment, the Mulla tumbled into the courtroom, his clothes flying, his beard ruffled, his turban awry. He stood beside the merchant and tidied himself a little as he caught his breath.

'My apologies, Your Honour,' he said. 'I was held up by my partner. He's a farmer, you see, and we share a wheat crop. We divide a small portion of the wheat between us and sell the rest. From it, we pay taxes and spend the rest on seed for the next crop. I have been wondering for a while now how to save a bit more for ourselves, and it has occurred to me that if we plant the burghul from our store cupboards instead, we can save all the money that we usually spend on fresh seeds.'

'Burghul? Don't you know that burghul is wheat that has been cracked and cooked, Mulla Nasruddin?'

'Indeed I do, Your Honour.'

'I take it you don't know much about farming, then!' said the judge scornfully. 'If you did, you would not expect fresh produce from cooked foods.'

'Ah,' the Mulla replied. 'Thank you, Your Honour. Because, you see, I have been puzzling, since I was last in your courtroom, how it was that cooked chickens produce eggs and cooked eggs produce chickens.'

Riding Politely

It was a very special occasion at the Madrasah. Mulla Nasruddin was famous for trying every trick he could think of to avoid giving sermons to his students at the college. He was happy to teach the boys at the school, but he drew the line at adults.

'They should know by now what I'm going to say,' he always said. 'And if they don't, then they're probably not interested. And if some of them know and others don't, those who do know can tell the others. They don't need me.'

But somehow, this time, he had promised to give a sermon to everyone. Given the slightest chance, though, he would still have wriggled out of it.

Everyone had heard of the Mulla's wisdom and his unusual ways, and a large crowd waited eagerly outside the Madrasah for him.

After a while, they saw a donkey in the distance, with the Mulla's turban just visible, bobbing about above the animal's back. As they got nearer, the students saw that the Mulla was sitting backwards on the donkey, facing its tail.

When the Mulla arrived at the Madrasah, he was welcomed warmly and everyone greeted him with respect. Then the Imam of the Madrasah asked him the question that was in everyone's mind.

'Khoja,' he said, 'your wisdom is acknowledged far and wide, and we wish to learn as much from you as we can because this is such a rare visit. May I be so bold as to ask why you were sitting backwards on your donkey?'

'Oh, that!' the Mulla laughed. 'You see these students following me? It seemed very rude to ride with my back to them. I was showing my appreciation by facing them.'

Inside the Coat

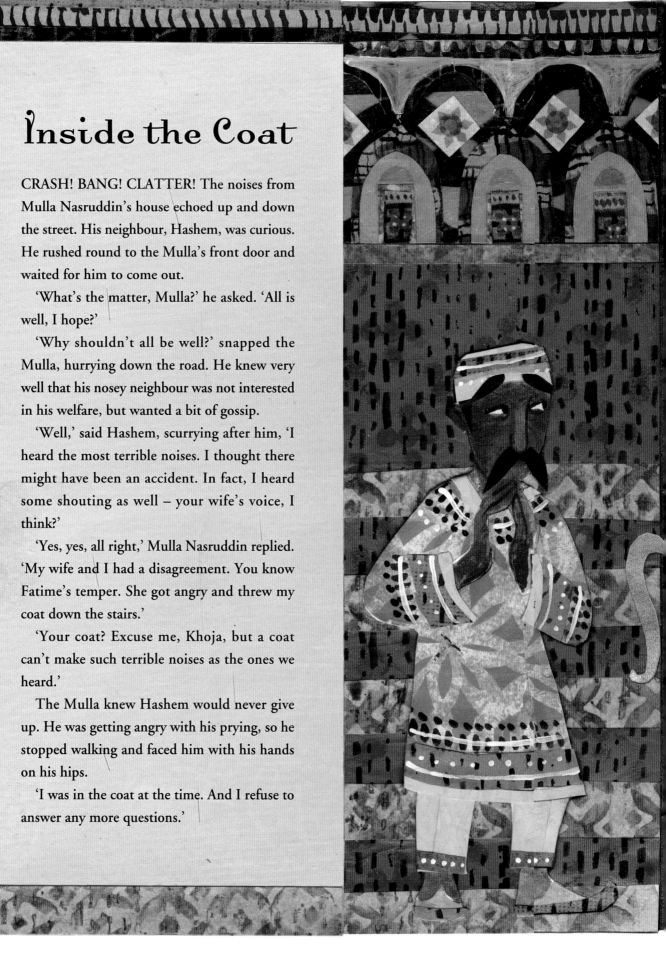

CRASH! BANG! CLATTER! The noises from Mulla Nasruddin's house echoed up and down the street. His neighbour, Hashem, was curious. He rushed round to the Mulla's front door and waited for him to come out.

'What's the matter, Mulla?' he asked. 'All is well, I hope?'

'Why shouldn't all be well?' snapped the Mulla, hurrying down the road. He knew very well that his nosey neighbour was not interested in his welfare, but wanted a bit of gossip.

'Well,' said Hashem, scurrying after him, 'I heard the most terrible noises. I thought there might have been an accident. In fact, I heard some shouting as well – your wife's voice, I think?'

'Yes, yes, all right,' Mulla Nasruddin replied. 'My wife and I had a disagreement. You know Fatime's temper. She got angry and threw my coat down the stairs.'

'Your coat? Excuse me, Khoja, but a coat can't make such terrible noises as the ones we heard.'

The Mulla knew Hashem would never give up. He was getting angry with his prying, so he stopped walking and faced him with his hands on his hips.

'I was in the coat at the time. And I refuse to answer any more questions.'

In the Highest Company

'For heaven's sake,' Mulla Nasruddin grumbled, getting out of his bed. 'It's three in the morning!' he grumbled some more when he answered the door.

'Emperor Taimur has summoned you,' said the men from the palace. 'He's worried about a serious question and insists that only you can calm his fears. Please get in the carriage.'

'Can't I at least get some decent clothes on?' the Mulla asked.

'The emperor cannot be kept waiting.'

The Mulla shrugged and climbed into the carriage. 'What Taimur wants, Taimur gets,' he mumbled, yawning. 'And who cares if some poor hard-working man's sleep is disrupted?'

The next thing he knew, they had arrived at the palace, where the guards shook him awake and led him before Emperor Taimur.

'Mulla Nasruddin,' the emperor said, 'do you know how worried I am?'

'Honestly, Sire? No, I don't,' the Mulla replied. 'It's very hard to think clearly when I'm so weary from lack of sleep.'

'That's a piffling matter, Mulla!' Taimur declared. 'My concerns are far more important.'

'Aren't they always, Your Majesty?' the Mulla murmured. But Taimur was too busy talking to hear.

'What will happen to me on the Day of Reckoning?' he groaned. 'Where will I go? Will I be given a seat in heaven? Or will I be sent to hell?'

The Mulla said nothing.

'Answer me, Khoja. I must have an answer or I won't sleep tonight.'

'I won't sleep tonight anyway,' thought the Mulla. 'The night will be nearly over by the time I reach home.' But Taimur was the emperor and he was demanding an answer.

Mulla Nasruddin rubbed his eyes and replied, 'Don't lose sleep over it, Your Majesty. I am sure you will have a seat of honour in the highest company, among the most powerful and brutal leaders of all time – Chengez Khan, Hulegu, Pharaoh and Nimrod. Now, shall we all go to sleep?'

Edible Bedding

Mulla Nasruddin lay in bed feeling more and more wakeful. His tummy rumbled and groaned, and deep inside he could actually feel pangs of hunger twisting and turning. He had made a big mistake.

'Next time,' he thought, 'I won't be so polite.'

The truth was, he had arrived late at his friend's house. It was past midnight, but his friend had given him a kind welcome and taken him up to a beautiful bedroom with a magnificent bed and wished him a very good night. Normally, the Mulla would have been delighted with this; but the trouble was, he had hurried to his friend's house as quickly as possible, and he had not had time for any dinner. And now, he was starving.

'Next time,' he vowed, 'if I'm hungry, I'll be bold and ask for food. I will never, ever put my poor starving belly through this agony again. Not ever.'

The Mulla turned over and covered his ears with the corners of his pillow to shut out the grumbling and moaning inside. He tossed and he turned. He got up and paced the room. He even fell down on his knees and prayed for relief. But nothing helped, so he got back into bed and started thinking.

'Shall I go and ask for something to eat?' he wondered.

Then he answered his own question. 'No, that would be ridiculous. You can't wake up your host in the middle of the night and demand food. That would be an insult.'

'Well, maybe I could go into the kitchen and help myself to a little something.'

'Of course you couldn't. That counts as stealing. You can't repay your host's hospitality by stealing his food.'

'It's not stealing. I'll just take a small piece of bread – and I'll tell him about it in the morning.'

'And what will he think then? That he's been a bad host who starved his guest. Is that what you want him to think?'

'Oh, for heaven's sake,' thought the Mulla, jumping out of bed again. 'I have to find some way of comforting my belly or I'll go mad.'

He pulled on his clothes and ran down to his friend's bedroom. Timidly, he knocked on the door. His friend appeared, rubbing his eyes.

'Forgive me, Khoja, is something wrong? Have I failed in my duties as a host?'

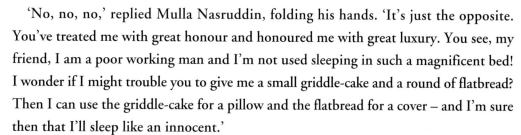

'No, no, no,' replied Mulla Nasruddin, folding his hands. 'It's just the opposite. You've treated me with great honour and honoured me with great luxury. You see, my friend, I am a poor working man and I'm not used sleeping in such a magnificent bed! I wonder if I might trouble you to give me a small griddle-cake and a round of flatbread? Then I can use the griddle-cake for a pillow and the flatbread for a cover – and I'm sure then that I'll sleep like an innocent.'

Share and Share Alike

The Mulla stood in front of a shop, eyeing a large bowl of freshly set yoghurt. It looked thick and creamy and cool, and the Mulla thought what a perfect meal it would make in the hot weather. But it was far too large for one man – and expensive, too. He felt in his pocket for the salad he had packed that morning before he left home. The heat had turned it into a wilted, watery mess of cucumber and tomatoes, and the Mulla wondered sadly if the olive oil he had packed would make it easier to eat.

'We could buy that yoghurt together and share it, Khoja,' said a voice in the Mulla's ear.

'Ah!' thought the Mulla, delighted. 'Fate has heard my plea.'

He turned around and saw Nedim from down the road in his village. Nedim was a fussy fellow, but the Mulla was hungry; and anyway, what could go wrong with something as simple as sharing a bowl of yoghurt? So he accepted Nedim's offer.

Nedim and the Mulla found a cool spot in the shade of a tree and set the bowl of yoghurt down on the grass. As soon as they were sitting down, Nedim leant forward and drew a line across the centre of the yoghurt.

'One half is yours, Khoja,' he said 'and the other is mine. This way we can make sure that the division is entirely fair.'

The Mulla didn't think that a division like this was necessary among civilised people, but it was too hot to argue, and so he held his tongue. Nedim, meanwhile, scrabbled around in his pocket and brought out a small packet.

'Khoja,' he said, 'I divided the yoghurt because I'm going to put some sugar in my half.'

'In your half?' Mulla Nasruddin asked, surprised. 'But yoghurt is liquid! Anything you put in your half is going to seep into my half. You might as well put the sugar in the middle for both of us to eat.'

'Oh no,' protested Nedim. 'I only have enough sugar for one – we never agreed to share the sugar, after all, only the yoghurt.'

'Fine,' said the Mulla, pulling out his olive oil. 'Then I won't share my oil with you.'

Nedim was horrified. He spread his hands over the bowl.

'You can't, Khoja! You'll ruin it.'

'That's my half of the yoghurt,' snapped the Mulla. 'I can do what I like with it. What's it to you?'

'But Khoja, you said yourself, a moment ago, that yoghurt is liquid and what you put in one half leaks into the other half.'

'In that case, put your sugar in the middle,' replied the Mulla, 'and I'll put away my oil.'

One-Legged Geese

Someone gave Mulla Nasruddin a very large goose.

'It's fit for the emperor!' said his wife. 'Let's give it to him as a gift.'

'What a brilliant idea, Fatime,' the Mulla exclaimed. 'That's exactly what I'll do.'

So they both set to work, grinding and grating and stuffing and roasting and turning and basting until the goose was a crisp golden brown. Then they lifted it onto a tray and covered it carefully with a piece of red cloth fringed with gold, and the Mulla set off on the road to the palace. The delicious aroma of the goose wafted out, leaving a fragrant trail behind him. As he wound through the small streets and onto the main road to the emperor's palace, people peeped from their windows and commented on the smell and asked about the huge parcel the Mulla was carrying. And with every word, he grew hungrier and hotter until at last he had to stop for a rest. So he found a large rock, set the goose down on it and plonked himself down beside it.

'My dear fellow,' he said, looking at the parcel, 'I've turned you into a rod with which to beat my back. If I had kept you for myself, I would have enjoyed your succulence and flavour – and I would have been sitting comfortably in my big chair, resting and thanking God for you. Instead, I'm slumped on a hot rock, on a hot day, with a very hot bird beside me, smelling of the pleasures of paradise – and I am not even allowed to sample it.'

He looked at the goose as if he was expecting an answer – then suddenly, before he fully knew what he was doing, he reached out, pulled off a drumstick and popped it in his mouth. Oh, what ecstasy! The taste exploded on his tongue. It was even more exquisite than he expected. He chewed slowly on it, allowing the flavours to linger, savouring its texture and succulence.

'Al-hamd-u-lilla!' he murmured. 'Praise God for this wonderful experience.'

He leapt to his feet, snatched up the goose and marched swiftly to the palace so that he would not be tempted to take the other leg.

Mulla Nasruddin strode solemnly past the guards at the gates, stalked past the attendants in the corridors and sailed past the courtiers. His back straight, his head held high, he walked right up to the emperor's private chamber behind the main

court, bowed low and placed the goose on a table. Then, ceremoniously, he swept off the gold-trimmed silk.

'A humble gift, Sire,' he said.

Taimur's nostrils twitched. He leant over to look at the golden mound of aromatic roasted meat. He sniffed once, then twice, then breathed in deeply. A joyful smile spread across his face.

'Bring the dish closer, Khoja,' he commanded.

Mulla Nasruddin held up the platter. Taimur opened his eyes. His eyebrows disappeared beneath his turban. His moustache twitched. He gasped.

'You dare to give me a half-eaten bird!' he spluttered.

'Half-eaten!' the Mulla spluttered back. 'What on earth do you mean, Your Majesty?'

'Look,' said the emperor. 'Surely you can see this goose only has one leg?'

'Alas, Your Majesty, who knows what lies behind God's plans? Geese are unlucky creatures. They often have just one leg.'

'I've eaten dozens of geese in my time – and I've never seen any with missing legs.'

'Look out of the window, Your Majesty,' the Mulla said.

Taimur looked out at the square where the military drills were held. A few geese stood lazily in the hot sun, with one leg curled up under their feathers to keep

cool. The Mulla breathed a sigh of relief.

'You see, Your Majesty,' he said.

'I do,' said Taimur. 'But I can't help wondering why I've never been served a one-legged goose before.'

Mulla Nasruddin looked thoughtful.

'I've heard, Sire, that palace chefs often remove the leg from birds that are to be cut up for stewing and attach them to the ones meant to be roasted whole. It creates symmetry and helps make the dish look more attractive.'

'I expect that explains it,' Taimur said, as the Mulla began to serve the goose to distract him.

Soon, the emperor was munching away at the perfectly roasted goose, while Mulla Nasruddin watched with great satisfaction, happy that his gift was being so well appreciated.

Outside, the soldiers were gathering for their drill. They formed into perfect lines, ready to start, and Taimur walked to the window to watch them.

BOOM! BOOM! BOOM! The cannon fired the start of the exercise. The startled geese dropped their legs to the ground.

'You lied to me, Khoja!' Taimur yelled. 'Every one of these geese has two legs!'

'Of course they do!' snapped the Mulla. 'And you'd grow four legs, if a cannon fired off that thunderous blast right over your head!'

Treading on God's Gift

'How beautiful the rain looks,' thought the Mulla, watching from his window. 'It washes everything clean and makes the flowers and trees grow. It is truly one of the most beautiful signs of God's grace.'

Just then, the peaceful view of the square with the rain pelting down on the flowers and trees was interrupted by a figure dashing through it. It was Enver, the Mulla's neighbour from two doors down. The Mulla stood up and leant forward a little.

'Enver! Enver, my friend! Why are you running?' he called as Enver got nearer.

'To get out of the rain, of course,' yelled Enver without stopping, swerving sharply towards his house.

'What a terrible, terrible shame!' Mulla Nasruddin called back. 'Rain is one of God's great gifts. I can't believe that people try to run away from it. No wonder God asks in His holy book: How many of My gifts will you deny?'

The Mulla noticed with satisfaction that Enver was slowing down even though the rain was getting heavier.

'A job well done,' he thought. 'I have managed to do some good.' And he settled back to watch the rain, until he became so mesmerised by the falling drops that he began to doze.

'Khoja!' called his friend Jamal, knocking at the window. 'The rain has let up for a bit. Do you fancy some coffee at Aydin's shop? I hear he has some fresh baklawa just in.'

The Mulla was never one to turn down fresh baklawa; and besides, Aydin served excellent coffee with just the right amount of cardamom. He heaved himself up and joined Jamal.

The baklawa was as fresh and crisp as he had hoped, and the coffee as rich. When he had finished, the Mulla looked out at the sky and saw that it was beginning to cloud over again.

'I think I'll get back home,' he said. 'It looks as if there's more rain coming.'

A bank of clouds had built up in the sky and, just as he stepped into the square, the first drops splattered the Mulla's face and shoulders. Quick as a lightning flash, he grabbed the folds of his trousers and sprinted across the square.

'Are you running away from the rain, Khoja?' called Enver's startled voice from his window.

'What does it look like to you?' replied the Mulla, crustily.

'I thought you said it was shameful to deny God's greatest gifts?'

And the Mulla replied, 'So it is. So it is, my friend. Now don't distract me – I mustn't tread on a single one of God's precious gift of raindrops.'

Tough Accounts

'Mulla Nasruddin,' said the Emperor Taimur one day, 'I hear that the Governor of Akshehir is a corrupt and greedy man. He must account for himself. What do you say?'

The Mulla knew very well that the emperor had heard of the governor's great wealth and wanted it for himself. 'I have never heard anything like that about the governor,' he replied.

'Silence!' bellowed Taimur. 'I am the emperor and I have spoken. Summon the governor to present his accounts.'

The governor arrived, with his accounts all written on a long piece of parchment. Taimur asked his scribe to read them out.

The Mulla could see Taimur was not really listening. He fiddled and fidgeted and they were only halfway through when Taimur yelled, 'I've heard enough! This man is dishonest. All his property and possessions will be taken from him and added to my treasury. And you, Governor, will eat these accounts, right here, in my presence. I hope that your dishonesty will give you indigestion.'

Mulla Nasruddin watched the poor man do as the emperor commanded. He chewed and swallowed, chewed and swallowed, until the Mulla could bear it no longer and gave him some water.

'You feel sorry for him, do you, Mulla?' Taimur said. 'Then perhaps you could take over his job?'

The Mulla protested. 'I know nothing about accounts, Your Majesty. I'm just a poor. . .'

'You are a judge,' the emperor interrupted, 'and you have been a merchant and a businessman in your time, not to mention a labourer. Of course you can do the job. I have complete faith in you.'

Mulla Nasruddin could do nothing about it if he wanted to keep his head, so he took up the post. Everyone congratulated him and told him how well he had done and how honoured he was. But the Mulla could not forget the gleam in Taimur's eye and the greed in his heart. And as the year came to its end, Taimur summoned the Mulla to the palace to present his accounts.

'Am I seeing things?' Taimur asked, laughing loudly. 'Are these accounts written on pastry?'

Mulla Nasruddin nodded. 'They are, Your Majesty.'

Taimur nibbled the corner of the accounts. 'This is excellent, flaky pastry,' he said. 'But why, Mulla?'

And the Mulla replied, 'Because, Sire, at my age I'd never manage to digest parchment.'

61

Glossary

Akshehir A city in western Turkey which has a shrine dedicated to Mulla Nasruddin. An international festival in honour of the Mulla is held here every year.

'Al-hamd-u-lilla' 'Praise be to God'

baklawa Crispy filo pastry filled with crushed pistachio nuts and soaked in honey or syrup and rosewater, popular all over the Middle East.

bath house A public bath where people paid to go in the days when very few houses had their own bathrooms. Bath houses were also enjoyable meeting places for local people.

burghul Dried, cracked wheat used in dishes such as salads, stews or served separately as an accompaniment to meat or vegetable dishes.

Bursa The capital of the province of Bursa, in north-west Turkey.

cardamom A fragrant spice. Its seeds are used to perfume food and drinks, especially coffee.

Chengez Khan A Mongol emperor (1154–1227) known for his ruthlessness.

Day of Reckoning The Last Day, or Day of Judgement, when, according to Muslim and Christian tradition, humans will be judged by their good or evil deeds.

Eid-ul-Adha The Festival of Sacrifice, an annual feast that celebrates the willingness of the Prophet Ibrahim (Abraham in the Bible) to sacrifice his son at God's command. Muslims mark the festival by sacrificing a goat or other domestic animal to give in charity to someone in need.

emperor The ruler of an empire.

Eskisheher A city and province in western Turkey.

flatbread A type of bread that is cooked without yeast.

griddle cake A simple, savoury, batter-based cake that is cooked on a griddle pan.

Hulegu A Mongol emperor (1217–1265) who wrought havoc in the Islamic countries.

Istanbul The old capital of Turkey, also known as Constantinople.

Khoja, Khwaja, Hoja, Hodja A term of respect, meaning 'master' or 'teacher'.

Konya A city in western Turkey, later associated with the famous Sufi teacher, Rumi.

Madrasah A school at which the Koran is traditionally taught to male students.

merchant A travelling businessman.

mosque A Muslim place of worship where people congregate for daily prayers.

Mulla A form of address for a learned Muslim or spiritual teacher.

Nimrod A mighty hunter from the Bible who challenged the power of God.

Pharaoh A merciless Egyptian ruler at the time of Moses.

piastre A small Turkish coin of little value.

'Salaam' A Muslim greeting which means 'peace'. The full greeting is 'As-salaam alaikum' meaning 'peace be upon you'.

Sivrihisar A town in western Turkey.

Sufi A type of Muslim committed to realising spiritual perfection.

Taimur A powerful emperor of Central Asia (1370–1405). He became famous as Tamerlane ('Taimur the Lame') after injuring his foot in battle.

Pronunciation Guide

Akshehir – AK-she-her

Al-hamd-u-lilla – al-HAM-du-lil-lah

Aydin – AYE-din

baklawa – bak-LAH-vah

Chengez Khan – chang-AYZ khan

Eid-ul-Adha – EED-ul-ad-hah

Ejaz – ey-JAHZ

Eskisheher – ES-ki-she-hir

Fatime – FAH-ti-may

Hashem – hah-SHEM

hodja – HO-jah

hoja – HO-jah

Hulegu – HOO-lay-goo

khoja – KHO-jah

khwaja – KHWA-jah

Madrasah – MAD-rah-sah

Nedim – ned-EEM

Pharaoh – FAY-roh

piastre – pee-AST-er

Sivrihisar – SIV-ree-hi-sahr

Taimur –TAY-moor

Sources

Classic Tales of Mulla Nasreddin, Houman Farzad (translated by Diane L. Wilcox), Mazda Publishers, Costa Mese, California, 1989.

The Exploits of the Incomparable Mulla Nasrudin, Idries Shah, Jonathan Cape, London, 1966.

Stories of the Hodja, Ziya Sak, Halk, Istanbul, 1968.

Tales of Mulla Nasruddin – For Children of All Ages, P. Raja, B.R. Publishing, Delhi, 1989.

Tales of Nasr-ed-Din Khoja, Henry D. Barnham, Nisbet & Co, London, 1923.

For Cameron Luke Cruz Shackle — S. H.

For my mother and father — M. A.

Illustrator's Note

When I was invited to illustrate a book about Mulla Nasruddin, my first step was to visit my local library to find out about him. Mulla Nasruddin is said to have been born in the 12th or 13th century in Afghanistan, Iran, Turkey, Tajikistan or Uzbekistan — it seems that everyone wants to claim him! I learnt that his stories are popular in central Asia, northern Africa, Greece, Russia, China, Pakistan, India, Indonesia and many other places.

The Mulla's multinational heritage gave me the opportunity to tap into the architecture, pottery, fabric, colours, landscapes and peoples of a rich variety of cultures. I found books on Indian and Persian miniatures (an ancient style of painting which was practised at the time of Nasruddin's birth); travel books on Turkey with pictures of towns the Mulla was said to have travelled through; beautiful tile and rug design books from all over Asia; and architecture books on palaces and mosques throughout the Muslim world. I also drew from the patterns, shapes and colours I knew from my childhood years in India.

I combed through the books with a sketchbook in my hand. I drew mosques, rugs, turbans, curly shoes, donkeys, minarets, pots, cypress and palm trees, skullcaps, arched doorways, tiles, moustaches and beards until I could do them all with my eyes closed.

I used what I had learnt in my research to craft the illustrations. I folded and cut patterns out of tissue paper and glued them to coloured paper. I created my own stamps using cut-up bicycle tyre inner tubes and rubber bands glued to wooden blocks. I covered coloured and origami paper with stamped patterns, and then I cut the shapes I needed until the Mulla had come to life amid a flurry of cut paper that filled my studio like confetti. By the time I finished, I felt that the Mulla had given me a gift from across the ages — a treasure chest of new ideas, patterns and designs to carry through to future projects.

Barefoot Books
294 Banbury Road
Oxford OX2 7ED

Barefoot Books
2607 Massachusetts Ave
Cambridge, MA 02140

Printed in China by Printplus, Ltd on 100% acid-free paper
Graphic design by Graham Webb, Warminster, UK
Colour reproduction by B & P International, Hong Kong

This book was typeset in Caliph and Garamond
The illustrations were prepared in collage

ISBN 978-1-78285-255-1

British Cataloguing-in-Publication Data: a catalogue record for this book is available from the British Library

Library of Congress Cataloging-in-Publication Data is available under LCCN 2010041261

1 3 5 7 9 8 6 4 2